HONOR AND PROTECT: A NOVELLA

BOOK FOUR IN THE HEROES OF EVERS, TEXAS SERIES

LORI RYAN

OTHER BOOKS BY LORI RYAN

The Sutton Billionaires Series:

The Billionaire Deal

Reuniting with the Billionaire

The Billionaire Op

The Billionaire's Rock Star

The Billionaire's Navy SEAL

Falling for the Billionaire's Daughter

The Sutton Capital Intrigue Series:

Cutthroat

Cut and Run

Cut to the Chase

The Sutton Capital on the Line Series:

Pure Vengeance

Latent Danger

The Triple Play Curse Novellas:

Game Changer

Game Maker

Game Clincher

The Heroes of Evers, TX Series:

Love and Protect

Promise and Protect

Honor and Protect (An Evers, TX Novella)

Serve and Protect

Desire and Protect

Cherish and Protect

Treasure and Protect

The Dark Falls, CO Series:

Dark Falls

Dark Burning

Dark Prison

Coming Soon – The Halo Security Series:

Dulce's Defender

Hannah's Hero

Shay's Shelter

Callie's Cover

Grace's Guardian

Sophie's Sentry

Sienna's Sentinal

For the most current list of Lori's books, visit her website:
loriryanromance.com.

CHAPTER ONE

L ily Winn didn't doubt herself very often, but right
about now seemed like a damned good time to start.
She'd seen plenty of birds flap their wings in a blind panic
against the bars of a cage, their fear palpable and real. She
was sure if she could crack open her chest and peek at her
heart, that's what it would look like right now. Clattering
against the bars of her ribcage trying to make a run for it.
When her friend had called and told her she suspected
there might be illegal dog racing happening in the area,
Lily's bright idea to go poking around abandoned farms or
ranchland in the area surrounding Evers, Texas had seemed
brilliant.

She gripped the empty dog collar and leash she carried
in her fist as a cover story and glanced around the property,
debating just how stupid it was to step out into the clearing.
Probably very. When she'd parked her Jeep out on the road
and hiked in, she'd figured anyone stopping her would buy

the story about looking for a lost dog. She was dressed for a hike, with khaki shorts, hiking boots, and her honey-blonde hair pulled back in a braid. She knew people saw her as the typical "girl next door" and she hoped that innocent look would play to her advantage here. The collar and leash were well-worn from use around her clinic. She thought the story would make a convincing one.

Now she wondered if anyone she ran into might shoot first and ask questions later. She hadn't lived in Texas very long, but her impression was that many of the natives around here might not spend a whole lot of time chatting up a stranger on their land. They'd shoot first and fast and without a lick of warning.

If she hadn't heard the whimpering just then, she might have remained frozen long enough to convince herself to turn back. If there was one thing Lily knew, it was the sound of an animal in pain. And it was the one thing she could never turn her back on—an animal in pain. Any animal.

With one final glance around, she stepped out of the woods and into the clearing that surrounded the old barn and its rundown corrals. The place looked abandoned, just as she'd been told. She hoped so. Because she didn't think she'd be able to carry off the lie about looking for her dog at this point. Not while her voice was shaking. Heck, her whole body was shaking.

Stupid, stupid, stupid, she chanted in her head as she pictured all of the horror movies with heroines who went into the dark room after hearing a noise no matter how much Lily yelled at the screen. No matter how stupid and foolish she told them they were, those horror movie chicks stepped forward into certain danger. As she was doing right now. *Great.* She was the stupid girl in the horror movie doing what everyone with half a brain knew you shouldn't.

Each breath sounded in her ears, jagged and raw, as she crossed the open space between corrals, moving toward the barn. Toward the source of the dog's cries. Closer and closer. Praying the barn was empty. Praying no one would pop out any minute. Or worse, simply shoot from where they stood. No, surely they would warn her first. Right?

She stopped in her tracks, listening to the sounds around her, blocking out the rasp of her own labored breathing. It wasn't the hike in that had done this to her. Even though it had been a half mile or more, she was fit. She'd taken it at a good clip. But this was fear, plain and simple. Maybe the bad guys wouldn't hear her gulps of air? Maybe it was only in her head.

The dog's cries came from around the side of the barn, drawing Lily's focus back to her goal. She edged toward the whimpering, creeping closer to the corner of the barn. If there was someone around that corner, she hadn't a clue how she'd handle that. She had no weapon. Nothing but her empty dog collar and leash and her cell phone shoved in her back pocket. The smart girl—the one who was still alive at the end of the horror movie—probably would have called for help. She'd have backed away and gone out to the car to wait for someone else to arrive.

But who would Lily call? She didn't have many friends

in town. She'd relocated to Evers to take over her grandfather's veterinary practice when he retired. He was housebound now after suffering a stroke. With her efforts to bring the practice up to date, she hadn't so much as poked her head out of the office.

She'd only met Mary Greene, who had warned her about the dog racing, because Mary brought rescue dogs into the clinic for discounted shots and spay and neuter. They chatted in the clinic but hadn't gotten together yet outside of it. She suspected Mary devoted most of her time to her full-time job and her rescue efforts. She likely didn't socialize all that much either.

It's not like Lily could call the police and tell them she needed help for a whimpering dog. They'd laugh at her. So, heart still pounding against the bars of its cage, she eased around the corner of the barn.

Nothing.

Not a person in sight, but also no sign of a dog. She could hear it more clearly now, and it must have smelled her presence because it began to yip loudly. A high-pitched, plaintive yip. She stepped out from the relative protection of the barn, such as it was, and scanned the area.

There. Lily didn't give thought to her safety as she rushed to the edge of a large ditch that looked like it had been dug by man, and not through any occurrence of nature.

"Oh no, no, no, no, no, no." She slipped and slid down the bank and wanted to close her eyes. Wanted to erase the sight before her. At least four other dogs lay in the ditch, but they were so clearly beyond her help, she didn't stop to check on them. She gritted her teeth as she ignored the flies that didn't seem the least bit bothered by her invasion, and made her way to the dog whose eyes were trained on her. There was pain in those eyes, but also hope. Lily quickly took in the injured back leg. It had been shot, the wound festering and necrotic. The leg was hanging, unusable. She knew without further inspection she'd need to remove it.

"This is going to hurt a little, baby girl, but I'll get you something to help with that soon."

Lily's hands worked quickly as she used her leash to make a makeshift muzzle for the dog. She didn't seem aggressive so far, but when Lily went to move her there'd be a lot of pain. A dog in pain can always bite. That was a lesson Lily had learned early and learned well. If she ever forgot it, she had the faint scars of a bite on her left wrist to remind her. The cream-colored dog had the markings of Saluki and Greyhound in her genes, with long, darker hair on her ears and tail, and a short coat covering her body. She had a thicker body than those breeds, though, so she might also have some Lab or something else in her. It was common practice in the world of underground dog racing to breed Greyhounds with other dog breeds to take advantage of the speed of the Greyhound's build, while making the mix sturdier to withstand the rigors of racing in empty fields. The dogs were called longdogs or lurchers, depending on the mix.

Lily used the thin button-up shirt she always wore over a tee at the office to tightly bind the leg. "Aren't you sweet, honey girl? Maybe that's what we'll call you," she crooned as the dog held remarkably still while Lily worked on her. "Honey," she said.

She stood and looked at the ground rising up in front of her. She would need to climb out of the ditch first, then try to drag the dog up the side. "I'm so sorry," she murmured, then stuck one foot into a divot in the mud wall in front of her and hoisted herself up and over the edge. The next part would suck for the dog. Royally suck. Lily laid on her stomach, shimmying forward as far as she could without falling into the hole again, and reached down toward Honey. She grasped her front legs, all the while keeping her focus on the soft trusting eyes of the incredible creature. She had to focus on that. If she focused on anything else, she'd see the dead eyes of the other animals in the pit. They had likely been tossed in here and shot. Honey was the only one who had held on long enough for Lily to have a shot at saving her.

She stumbled under the weight of the dog when she first lifted her, but once hoisted in her arms, it wasn't so bad. Lily was strong and used to moving animals whose full weight hung limp under sedation. Sure, she typically had help, and didn't have to walk half a mile, but she wasn't about to leave Honey here and risk whoever had shot those dogs coming back to finish her off. Walking as quickly as she could, Lily cut back through the woods and out to the road. She needed to get Honey back to her clinic. She'd lose the leg, for sure. If Lily got lucky, though, maybe it wasn't too late to save Honey's life.

CHAPTER TWO

Carter Jenkins pulled open the door to Winn Animal Clinic and smiled when he saw Bea Bishop at her usual post behind the reception desk. Like her sister, May, Bea brought a smile to the faces of most people who met her, and he knew she used her naturally mothering way whenever someone was upset or worried about a beloved pet. She'd used it on him a number of times when he'd brought Memphis in. The German Shorthaired Pointer who had been Carter's hunting partner for the better part of ten years was declining bit by bit. Of course, someone would have to let the dog know that. Memphis was convinced he was still two years old, and that attitude led to a lot of twists, bumps, bruises... Well, overall, just trouble. Plain and simple.

"Hey there, Carter. I didn't think you had an appointment today," Bea said, glancing at her desk. The office had used paper calendars for scheduling when Dr. Winn was in charge. Now that the new Dr. Winn—the blonde-haired, brown-eyed girl who made Carter think of that song anytime she smiled his way—was in charge, they were moving everything to computers. Carter had heard she would be expanding the space soon, too, building a kennel to offer boarding and grooming. He wasn't sure how that would go over. Most of the town was made up of good old boys who'd just as soon leave out a big bowl of food and water and put the dog in the yard when they went on a trip, but he hoped it worked out for her. If for no other reason than he'd get to keep looking at those eyes and seeing if he could get her to aim that smile his way.

"No appointment, Bea," he said with a smile as he crossed to her desk. He glanced at the hallway behind her, hoping to spot Dr. Winn. "I'm just picking up Memphis's meds. I called last week about his heartworm pills, but haven't been able to get here until now."

"I bet you're busy. Is Sheriff Davies getting ready for his wedding? He must be fixin' to take off pretty soon, I guess." As she spoke, she opened a cabinet and pulled out a small bag with his receipt already stapled to it. That was another thing Lily Winn had put into place. She kept a credit card on file so her staff could get things ready in advance. It wasn't exactly how the town of Evers was used to doing things, and Carter would bet she'd had some pushback on it, but it worked for his schedule when he was busy.

Carter couldn't help the smile that crossed his face at the mention of his boss. He'd watched tough-as-nails Sheriff John Davies take call after call about flower choices, cake flavors, and a disaster with bridesmaids' dresses that had been ordered in the wrong color over the last six months. Carter had to admit, he'd had more than a few laughs over it. "He's officially on vacation starting today. Katelyn convinced him to take almost a week off leading up to the wedding so they could get things ready, and then another ten days after the wedding for their honeymoon."

"Ah, yes," Bea laughed. "The glamping trip. I heard about that. What I haven't quite figured out—" she leaned in, although Carter wasn't exactly sure who she was afraid might hear them, "—is what *glamping* is."

He tipped his head back and laughed. "It's not the kind of camping I'm used to, that's for sure." Carter and his brothers had been raised in Evers by a father who believed in teaching his sons to live off the land. Before he was ten years old, Carter could follow almost any animal track, catch fish from a river with his bare hands or a rod he'd made himself out of whatever he could find in the woods, and hunt with either a rifle or a bow. If forced to, he could live in the woods, relying on nothing but the land for food and shelter.

He continued on, answering Bea's question. "It's glamorous camping—oversized tents with queen-sized beds and satin sheets. Cabins with outdoor showers built into the side of a mountain. That kind of thing."

Bea shook her head. "Then why camp at all?" There was laughter but also a little bewilderment in her tone.

"You got me," he answered with a shake of his own head, but a little part of him thought if a gorgeous woman had fallen for him the way Katelyn had fallen for John, he'd probably happily sleep in any cabin she suggested.

"Well, now, I suppose with John off on his honeymoon, you'll be taking over for him?"

Carter nodded, and answered with a "yes, ma'am," but no more. He was still a bit uncomfortable with his recent promotion to Chief Deputy Sheriff. He was prouder than hell, but it somehow seemed a little too much like bragging to speak of it.

"Then you're just who I need to speak to."

Carter's head whipped around at the sound of a voice he'd recognize anywhere, only it sounded different right now. Lily Winn's usual melodious, kind tone—the one that always seemed warm and gentle, even as it seemed to effortlessly heat his blood—was missing. In its place was anger. An anger that matched the hands-on-hips posture she'd just taken in the hallway behind Bea. She looked less put together than she usually did. Not that she was one of those women who needed to doll herself up with fancy clothes and a protective layer of crap on her face. Lily always looked fresh-faced and casual, like she was ready for a hard day's work. He liked that about her. But right now, she looked like she'd just run a marathon. She had one of those little surgical caps on her head—images of puppies played along its edge, because she never seemed to wear anything that was plain and boring—but there were a few tendrils of hair slipping out.

"That was a long surgery, Doc," Bea said, using the same nickname for Lily that she'd used for Lily's grandfather over the years. Carter had to bury images of him and Lily playing doctor anytime Bea said it.

"It was," Lily said, eyes still glittering with anger. Those eyes were pinned to him as though the anger were aimed his way.

"Surgery?" he asked, figuring he might as well try to figure out why he was in the hot seat. She'd said something about needing to speak to him as the Chief Deputy Sheriff. He kept his face open and neutral, waiting for her to let him know what was going on.

"Yes. Emergency amputation. I just had to take the leg of a dog that was shot by scum who were using her for underground racing. She was the lucky one. There were four others who didn't make it. My guess is they weren't running as fast as their dirtbag owners would like them to anymore, or maybe they were trying to breed them and they weren't producing. Who knows? It doesn't matter why. What matters is they were thrown out like trash in the bottom of a ditch."

Carter could see the emotion brimming beneath the mask of anger on her face. She was quickly shifting from anger to despair and he had a feeling she might be crying if she weren't so furious. He didn't blame her. What she was describing was horrific. He glanced over his shoulder at the waiting room, happy to see it empty, and nodded toward her office door down the hall.

"Why don't we go somewhere quiet and you can tell me what's going on?"

As Carter listened to Lily tell him about searching for

evidence of underground dog racing, he had to clench his teeth against the urge to reach out and shake the woman. What was she thinking, going off on her own like that? Underground dog racing wasn't illegal in Texas, but the gambling that went with it was. They also often used a live animal lure, which *was* illegal in Texas. It was hard to prove, though, so unfortunately it wasn't something that was prosecuted very often.

"Lily," he said as calmly as he could under the circumstances. "What were you thinking? You could have been hurt. Or worse. These aren't exactly the nicest people. Rabbit running is a nasty business. You can't just run off half-cocked and take matters into your own hands."

He knew it was a mistake as soon as he said the words, but there wasn't any taking them back. Her eyes flashed at him again, as fury coursed through her little frame. Well, she could rage at him all she wanted. He was right. She was wrong. There was no denying it.

He was shocked when she stood, shoving herself up from her desk abruptly. "Follow me."

She was halfway out the door before he followed, shaking his head. Didn't she get it? This wasn't a game she could just stop playing when things got too hot.

Lily stopped in front of a wall made up of four small cages across the top, three medium ones in the center, and two large on the bottom. The bottom right-hand cage held a medium-sized dog, clearly still groggy from surgery. Layers of colorful bandages covered her hind end where Lily had had to remove the leg, and he could see that an area much larger had been shaved. He couldn't imagine the size of the wound left beneath the wraps. The dog opened her eyes and gave a very soft flap of the end of her tail, but other than that showed no acknowledgement that they were there.

"This is what's happening to these dogs, Deputy Jenkins. If I hadn't gone out there today, Honey would have died a horrible drawn-out death. Four others didn't make it. Who knows how many other dogs those barbarians have and what they're doing to them."

He didn't explain to her that underground dog racing was rarely prosecuted. Nor did he look very long at the sweet, trusting eyes of the dog before him. Instead, he looked at the hope and belief in the eyes of the woman next to him. She believed in him, believed he could and would do something to stop this.

She was right that whoever had done this had broken the law by shooting the dogs. If he could manage to link anyone back to the crime, that is. It was a state felony to kill an animal like that. If they were using live bait or gambling during the races—which, ironically, *he* could damned near put money on—those were another set of crimes all together. The issue was getting any kind of proof. He couldn't really justify spending state funds on ballistics and fingerprint testing for an animal cruelty case, when they were so underfunded for things like murder and rape.

Carter bit back a sigh and shook his head. "Promise me you won't go back out there. That you'll leave this to me."

"You'll do something about it?" she countered, squaring off, hands going back to her hips.

"Yeah, I'll do something about it." He didn't know what, but he would. He was in charge of the county for almost three weeks. He'd damned well make sure to do all he could to put a stop to the racing, but more importantly, to be sure Lily didn't get hurt trying to take care of it on her own. Not on his watch. "I'll take care of it, Lily."

For a brief second, Carter let himself play out the fantasy that had been tickling the edges of his mind since he'd first met Lily Winn. In his mind's eye, he reached out and pulled her into his arms, gently easing that strong, gorgeous body into his to see if they fit. He knew they would. They'd fit together *perfectly*. He didn't know why he knew it, but he did. Once he had her pressed thigh to thigh, hip to hip, and chest to chest against him, he'd frame that sweet face with his hands and delve into the mouth that always seemed to tantalize and tease.

When she opened to him, he'd nibble at her plump lips. He'd do all he could to elicit a moan from her, knowing he'd be primed with need for her in the blink of an eye.

Then her hand was on his arm, and Carter had to shake himself out of the stupor he'd dropped into. She wasn't living the same fantasy he was. In fact, her touch was all business. It was clinical as she patted him on the arm and thanked him, calling him Deputy Jenkins instead of Carter. Because that's what he was to her. An official. Someone whose help she needed. Nothing more. He'd do well to remember that. But damn, that fantasy was hard as hell to resist.

He cleared his throat. "No problem. I'll look into it."

CHAPTER THREE

Carter paused at Berta Silver's desk in the building that housed the sheriff's office in downtown Evers. Berta was indispensable to the office. She ran things, acted as dispatcher much of the time, and generally kept all of them in check. She was also able to get any information they needed faster than most of the deputies could.

"Berta, can you see if you can find a list of ranch or farm properties that are empty or abandoned? Maybe properties facing foreclosure? Anything isolated with a lot of land." Lily had given him the location of the property where she'd found the dogs. He'd already gone out there with Danny Widen, another deputy, and found the dogs in the ditch, as Lily had described. There'd been little else there. They found two broken dog crates and a couple of muzzles that had apparently been left behind as well. Both of those things could point to either racing or fighting. The dogs weren't the typical breeds used for fighting, so his guess was racing. Illegal rabbit running—letting dogs loose to run after a rabbit in a field and bet on which one caught it first—was pretty big in the area. Unfortunately, they didn't find anything that could substantiate an arrest for gambling, much less help identify who was using the dogs.

He and Danny had taken pictures of the dogs in the pit and collected the remains, but there wasn't going to be a budget for running a ballistics match against the bullets in the carcasses. Sad as it was, the county just didn't have the means for that type of thing when so much had to go to investigating and prosecuting crimes against people.

Berta picked up a pen and jotted a note. "Sure thing, boss."

Carter winced. "I think we can forego the *boss* title, seeing as this is temporary." She only laughed at him and went right on as though he hadn't said anything.

"Whatever you say, boss. Looking for anything in particular, other than isolated and likely empty?"

"That's all I've got for now."

"Heard from John yet? He getting tired of playing house and itching to be back at work?" Berta chuckled at her own humor. Not many could accuse the sheriff of playing house, but Berta could get away with it.

Carter shook his head, but a smile played at the corners of his mouth. "Last I heard, he was happily double-checking flower orders and picking up tuxes."

She huffed out what he supposed was meant to be laughter. "I never thought Sheriff Davies would be trussed up in a tux voluntarily, much less dealing with flowers and frou-frou wedding plans."

Carter forced a smile, but the pang of envy he felt made the smile taste bitter on his lips. "Love'll do that to a man, Berta. Love'll do it."

As he walked away, his mind flashed to the tempting veterinarian who seemed completely oblivious to him. Well, oblivious as far as his feelings went. He'd have to see what he could do to change that. Carter had never been a man to sit and hope for things to go his way, and he sure as hell wasn't going to rely on hope with Lily.

CHAPTER FOUR

Three days later, Lily kept her eyes on the dog at her feet. If she looked at the man standing next to her, she'd, well...she'd have to see the man standing next to her. A man whose almost-black hair and square, beard-covered jaw gave her the strangest urge to reach out and run her hand down the side of his face. What was that about? A man whose eyes she was dying to decipher, because she'd be damned if she could figure out if they were hazel or gray, or maybe even green. They seemed to change every time she glanced his way. He was tanned from the sun, with the body of someone who obviously spent time being physical instead of sitting behind a desk.

And that made her like him all the more. Only she couldn't like him. She. Would. Not.

So her eyes stayed glued to Honey, who raised her head and flapped her tail hopefully.

"Did you guys find anything that can help you arrest the people who did this?"

Carter shook his head. "Nothing yet. We collected what little evidence there was at the site you found, but there wasn't much to go on. I'm looking into other empty properties, but I don't have anything yet."

Lily shivered, and it wasn't related to the temperature. "I just can't help thinking that these guys must have a lot of dogs, and who knows when they'll kill or torture another one."

Carter turned toward her. "How do you figure?"

"If they could so easily shoot five of them at a time—" She didn't finish. The lump in her throat wouldn't let her. Lily looked up and found Carter watching her. *Look away, Lily. Eyes on the dog. Eyes on the dog.*

She cleared her throat and went back to filling him in on Honey's progress. "So, she's doing well, moving around with assistance—"

"Assistance?"

"Sure." Lily nodded and glanced at him briefly before looking away again. His eyes were on her. Shouldn't he be watching the dog? That's what he was here for. She swallowed and kept going, desperately trying to ignore the nerves he brought out in her. It wasn't fair. She was a professional. She had an advanced degree. Actually, two of them. She wasn't a little girl with a case of puppy love. She shouldn't have to fight the butterflies in her stomach to give him the rundown on Honey's medical condition.

She cleared her throat and refocused on his question.

"We use a strap under her belly to help lift her as she walks. She's able to go out for potty breaks with it, and as she gains confidence and balance, we ease up on the support until she's no longer relying on the strap."

He nodded. "Smart."

Maybe if she kept talking she could ignore the fact that his arm had just brushed against hers. Because, cripes, that shouldn't have felt so dang good. "She'll need to go to a foster home soon, though. She's ready for it and I want to get her out of the clinic. I mean, not because it's a problem to have her here. It's not. It's just that it can be stressful. All the other dogs coming in and out, the cats, the noise. All of it can be a bit much for a dog trying to recover long term."

Now she was babbling. Great.

"She can't go home with you?" Carter asked, turning to her again.

"No. I live too far away. I wouldn't be able to make it home to check on her, take her out to the bathroom. She needs someone to stop and check in every few hours for now. It's okay," she assured him. "I'll ask around. Someone will be able to help, I'm sure."

Lily actually didn't have any pets at the moment, which was weird for a veterinarian, but she'd been working her tail off while in school and now here to establish herself. She wanted to keep Honey, and actually thought she might adopt her if no one else stepped forward. For now, though, Honey needed out of the clinic environment and into a home where she could get the care she needed. Lily's home just wasn't going to meet her needs for the time being. And Lily needed to think of Honey's needs, not her own.

"I can take her."

"What? I mean, you *can*?"

Carter nodded and she had to admit she was stunned. That was unexpected. In fact, she'd been a little surprised that he'd showed up to check on the dog in the first place.

"Yeah, I live nearby, and my house is only a few minutes from the station, so it isn't a problem to swing by and take her out when I'm on patrol. I can also get a few of the other deputies to help out. We'll get her covered between all of us."

"Wow, that would be great. If you're sure. Are you sure? Because, I mean, that would be great."

Now he was laughing at her. "Great," he said, his grin telling her he was teasing her just a little bit. "I do have one requirement, though."

"You do?"

He nodded solemnly, holding her gaze. "That you have coffee with me."

"Coffee with you?"

"Yes. Coffee with me."

"Coffee with you?"

He cocked his head and laughed. "Is that confusing somehow? It'll be simple, really. We'll just meet up, walk down to the diner. Grab some coffee. Maybe a piece of pie."

She clamped down on her lips, biting them from the inside to stop herself from saying "pie" back to him in the dimwitted, parroting manner she'd fallen into in the past few minutes. She wasn't a stupid woman. Yet all the evidence was pointing in that direction right now.

"I don't date," was what came out when she finally did release her lips. Good. That was good. Direct. Firm. Final.

"Good. Because coffee doesn't count as a date."

She didn't know what to think of that. Could the man really just want to have coffee? Maybe he wanted to ask more about dog racing or to find out more about taking care of Honey and what it would entail. Maybe he was trying to kill two birds with one stone, grabbing a coffee break and snack while he got the information he needed from her.

"Okay, I'll get my purse." She turned to walk away, but was stopped by his answer.

"Now? You want to go now?" Now he was the one who looked stunned and Lily began to feel like this was the most bizarre conversation she'd ever had.

"Um, yes?" Because suddenly, it seemed very important to get this over with. To take care of the coffee commitment and finish this—whatever *this* was—once and for all. Then she'd get some semblance of her sanity back. Some smidgen of control over her emotions, her thoughts, and most importantly, her foolish girly parts that were trying to stage a mutiny against her no dating policy. A policy she wanted to keep firmly in place. No, not *wanted* to keep in place. A policy she *would* keep firmly in place. "Yes. Now would be great." *Ugh. Again with the "greats".*

"Great," he said as his grin stretched wide, and she knew the laughter in his eyes was aimed at her.

CHAPTER FIVE

C arter smiled to himself as he walked Lily back to her office after their coffee "non-date." It was a date. She just didn't know it yet. He could deal with that. He would give her space and time. When he'd asked her why she didn't date, she said she'd had all the romance she could handle. Apparently, not one, not two, but three men had told her they loved her before leaving her. She'd had three long-term relationships, complete with flowers, candlelight dinners, and whispered words of love and forever. In each case, that love hadn't proven strong enough. For one reason or another, the men had "changed their minds," as she put it.

When she told him, she acted as though she was over the guys, and she might very well have been. He could tell she wasn't over the hurt though. Maybe simply the surprise of it. The surprise when one after the other left, despite telling her they would never go. When one after the other said they didn't love her anymore, or that their love—*her* love—just wasn't enough. He didn't know what was wrong with those idiots, but he did know one thing. Moving quickly wouldn't be an option with her. That was fine with him. He didn't need speed. He was perfectly happy to take his time, to get to know her and let her see she could trust him. To build that trust with one simple act after another. One kiss at a time. One day at a time. Whatever it took. Because the more time he spent with her, the more he liked her. The more he wanted to be with her.

They'd had more in common than he thought they would. She valued family above all else. Christmas dinner at home was more than just an obligation to her. When she spoke of her parents and siblings, the love in her eyes was apparent. It didn't stop there. She loved to hike and mountain bike, just like him. He even liked the way her version of dressing up was a pair of jeans—jeans his hands were aching to relieve her of—and a cute camisole. He was willing to bet she didn't own a pair of Loui-boo-frou-frou or whatever-they-were-called shoes, unlike the woman he'd dated last year. A sweet, beautiful woman, but one he couldn't connect with at all. Not like Lily.

"So Honey will be ready to go home in a couple of days?" he asked as they approached the front of her clinic.

"Uh huh," she said, and he had to stifle a laugh at the way she was all but sprinting to the door in her desire to leave. If it weren't for the other desire he could see in her eyes and the chemistry arcing between them, he might be offended. Acting like she wanted to be away from him right now didn't mean anything. She wanted him as much as he wanted her.

"Good, so Friday then? I can pick her up after I take you out to dinner."

"What? But, but, what?" It was fun making her sputter.

"Dinner. Two people, eating food. More talking. Much like what we just did," he said, turning back toward the diner briefly. "Only it will involve more food and be a bit later in the day. Then we'll swing by the clinic. I assume you have a key to get in after hours?" He didn't wait for an answer. He just answered her sputtering with a smile and went on. "We'll pick up Honey and you can help me get her settled in at my place."

Her eyes went round and her face flushed. She was moving her mouth as if she couldn't quite make the words come out despite wanting to, but there was heat there also. Heat and interest. She wanted to come over to his house.

"I can't come to your house!"

He tipped his head back and laughed. She was really cute, he had to give her that. He was about to reassure her that all he wanted was her help getting Honey settled in, but Alton Crawford interrupted them. He'd just come from inside the clinic and had apparently overheard some of their conversation.

"You're taking the dog, Deputy Jenkins?"

Carter would bet he and Lily wore matching looks of surprise when they turned to the lawyer. Carter extended his hand, more out of habit than anything, and Alton gripped it briefly, before reissuing his question.

"You're taking the racing dog? The one that was shot?"

Carter ignored the question. "What's your interest in Honey, Alton?"

Alton Crawford was a prominent lawyer in the small town. He and his wife were active in the community and the largest church in town, and Carter couldn't begin to imagine why he'd be so interested in Honey and where she went.

"Nothing, nothing." Alton's denial was too hurried. Too strong. "I just came by to drop off some papers for Lily and saw the poor thing. Awful, what someone did to her. It's a miracle you found her and saved her in time, Lily. Just a miracle."

Lily glanced at Carter before answering and he found himself placing a hand to her back. "I was out hiking. It wasn't a miracle at all. Just chance."

Alton nodded. "Well, sure. Sure. Anyway," he turned to Carter again, "you're taking the dog?"

Carter didn't answer and Lily cut in. "Alton, you said you brought paperwork by. Does that mean the landlord is willing to lease additional space to me?"

"Oh, yes. It's all set. You just need to sign and write a check. He'll give you the first two months' rent free since you're taking the buildout on by yourself. I still say let him do the buildout and spread out the payments each month, but you seem to be set on doing it your own way."

Carter smiled when Lily raised her brows at the lawyer, stopping him in his tracks. He couldn't help but be impressed by the way she took him on, clearly making her business decisions where she saw fit.

"Yes, well..." Alton moved past them on the walk, clearing the way to the door for Carter and Lily to enter. "I'll need the papers back with the check by close of business tomorrow."

"You got it," Lily answered, and Carter was happy to see a smile break over her face. She was proud to be expanding her business, and he was happy for her. She should be proud.

As they walked away, he watched Alton. The man glanced over his shoulder several times, telling Carter his hunch was right. Something was up. Alton's interest in Honey was strange. And strange didn't set well with Carter. Especially when it involved Lily.

CHAPTER SIX

"You *shot* them?" Alton whispered, even though his office door was closed.

"Of course I shot them," Jenk Wilson answered through the line, with a sneer so plain in his voice, it wasn't hard for Alton to picture it on his face. They'd gone to school together back in the day, but each had gone his separate path until they'd partnered up a year ago. Alton's path had included a top-tier law school. Jenk's education came care of the penitentiary system, and it was a lot more limited than Alton's. But he was street smart, and he knew dog racing. Knew how to train the dogs, how to draw in the crowds without drawing the attention of the police, and how to make them both money doing it. When Alton's lifestyle first began to creep ahead of his income, he hadn't worried overly much. When it had bolted forward by leaps and bounds as his income began to decline with each year in this pissant town, Alton had gone along with Jenk's scheme. Dog racing. Only he hadn't planned on dogs being shot.

Before Alton could answer him, Jenk continued. "What did you think I did with them when they were done? You think I have some nice retirement home out in the country for them? If they aren't running or breeding, or earning their keep in some way, they need to go."

"Well, you didn't bury the bodies deep enough, Jenk." Alton swallowed his unease at the thought of shooting an animal in cold blood. They needed to do damage control now. "The local vet found the bodies when she was hiking. One of the dogs survived. She had to cut off its leg, but the damned thing is still alive. She's got the deputy sheriff involved."

Jenk grunted. "Doesn't matter. Dog racing isn't illegal, Crawford, so you can pull your panties outta your damned ass crack. No one cares if you're running a few dogs."

"They'll care about the gambling. That's plenty illegal. And they'll care about the rabbits those dogs are chasing. About the dogs you're shooting. If I'm connected to any of that, prosecution won't matter at all. It'll ruin me, Jenk, and I'm not about to let that happen."

Another grunt through the line was all he heard before the phone cut out. Alton muttered a curse and swiped at his brow as he sank back into his chair. He could not let this get out. Jenk might not care about his reputation, but reputation was everything to Alton. Everything. His would be shot to hell if anyone got wind of this.

CHAPTER SEVEN

Lily was in a state all day Friday, and it wasn't a good one. She wanted dinnertime to come, and didn't at the same time. She knew she should just tell Carter she couldn't go to dinner with him. That she would help him get Honey settled at his house, but that going out together wasn't an option. She didn't date. It was that simple.

And yet... She sighed. And yet, she wasn't able to resist feeling the littlest bit of excitement at the thought of spending more time with Carter. The man made her laugh. She liked talking to him, liked hearing his stories. She liked the way he looked at her and listened, and the way he made her feel like she was the only person in the room. The only person he wanted to talk to.

The way her body responded to him couldn't be ignored either, but that was the problem, wasn't it? She didn't want there to be any attraction between them. Didn't want him to make her want things, but he absolutely did.

Because let's face it, the man was hot. And he used it to his advantage. Not in a way that made her think he'd push her for something she didn't want. In fact, he was doing all he could to show her he'd wait. That didn't mean he couldn't tell her breath caught every time he stepped close to her. He seemed to know the effect he had when his hand brushed her arm or when he leaned close to whisper something to her.

"Lily?"

Lily jumped when Bea walked into the exam room where she was finishing up a client note. "Yes?"

"Ryan Crawford is here to pick up the lease agreement for his father. He said you were expecting him."

Lily glanced at her watch, realizing with surprise that it was five thirty already. Time would be tight to change and be ready when Carter picked her up in half an hour. She refused to do much to get ready for a date she didn't want to go on, but hadn't been able to stop herself from bringing cute jeans that fit better than the scrubs she wore every day, paired with a halter top that showed off her arms.

"Can you send him to my office? I'll be there in just a minute."

Rushing to wrap up her notes, she moved down the hall to her office. She'd met Ryan Crawford a couple of times since moving to town, but usually saw him at his father's office. Apparently, he was about to begin his third year of law school and planned to join his father's practice when he graduated. He was a nice-looking man with a fairly unre-markable face, and a smile that seemed genuine and easy.

Stacking him up next to Carter, which her mind's eye couldn't help but do, he paled in comparison. He was a couple of inches taller than Lily, where Carter stood over six feet tall. Ryan had none of the rugged strength and natural sex appeal Carter had. He was simply...nice-looking.

"Hi, Ryan. Sorry to keep you waiting. I've got the papers here for you. Thank you so much for coming to pick them up. I had hoped to bring them down to your dad yesterday, but the day got away from me faster than I thought it would."

He took the offered papers and smiled. "No problem. I heard you had some excitement around her lately. Everything from pulling dogs out of ditches to saving Francine Moller's prized show poodle yesterday when you performed an emergency C-section to deliver her puppies." He whistled. "I'll bet she was a Nervous Nellie in the waiting room, huh?"

Lily smiled. She'd practically had to physically remove Francine from the surgery suite. The prized poodle and her two puppies were safe. It had been a good day.

"It's been an interesting few days, to say the least," Lily said, avoiding the topic of other people's pets. "I didn't think a small-town veterinary practice would be so action-packed, but it's been a nice surprise."

He nodded and smiled at her again and she got the feeling he was working up to something. There was a lot of smiling going on. "So, Lily, I was wondering if I could take you to dinner sometime?"

"Oh, uh—" She mentally swatted at the image of Carter's face in her head. Why did he keep popping up there? She bit back a sigh and looked at Ryan. Maybe he was the answer. In reality, she didn't want to date Ryan any more than she wanted to date Carter. But Ryan was safe. She wasn't wildly aroused when he was around. She'd probably enjoy dinner out with him, without feeling like she might lose her heart the way she did with Carter.

Sadly, her mouth wasn't on board with the plan, because she found herself politely declining and making excuses. "I'm sorry, Ryan, I'm not really dating right now. I mean, I'm just focusing on the business and trying to get settled in and that kind of thing."

His smile didn't falter in the least. "Sure. Maybe in a few weeks, then?"

"Maybe," she said, returning the smile, but she had a feeling her heart wouldn't be interested in a few weeks either.

Of course, that wasn't at all how she felt three hours later when she and Carter had come back from dinner, and were getting Honey settled into his house. Lily not only had a wonderful time at dinner with him, she'd forgotten all of her objections to dating over the course of their time together. They sat side by side on the floor of Carter's living room, watching Honey snuggle into the soft, cozy bed he'd bought her as Lily strained to remember all the reasons she was dead-set against this going anywhere.

She could do this. She'd just remember the words of all the men who had let her down before. Of all the men who'd disappointed her. All the men who'd left. *I just don't think this is going to work for me.* That's what Keith had said when he left her after a year and a half of living together. After all the words of love and promises together, a simple *I just don't think this is going to work for me* was what she'd been left with.

Intent on saying goodnight, since Honey was clearly in good hands, she turned to Carter. She sucked in a breath and knew her lips had parted, despite her efforts to clamp them shut. Because Carter was watching her. And *heated gaze* didn't even begin to describe the look in his eyes. A second later, when their mouths met, she was mortified to realize that it might have been her to initiate the kiss, not him. And here she thought she would be strong, fend off his advances, reject him. Instead, she had leaned in and closed the space between them, not only touching her lips to his, but also running the tip of her tongue along his lower lip. Tasting him.

He groaned as his arms came around her, and Lily lost her breath when he commandeered the kiss, taking it to another level entirely. *Incendiary* was the word that came to mind. Carter somehow pulled her closer, his body pressing to hers as he slanted his head and deepened their connection. He nibbled, licked, sucked, kissed, and teased moan after moan from her. She answered back, pushed herself farther into him, reveling in how hard his body was. She caught his lower lip in her teeth and tugged gently, loving the low growl she earned in response.

Though she hated to admit it, if Carter hadn't pulled

back, she couldn't be sure she would have. That really ticked her off. She'd been so sure she could be strong.

"I don't date," she whispered as he watched her face.

"So you've said. I have to tell you, though, this is beginning to feel awfully *date-ish* to me. But I'm out of practice. Maybe we should try it a few more times. Maybe it's not what we think it is."

"And you think a few more dinners will help us figure it out?"

"Absolutely."

Lily laid her forehead on Carter's chest and groaned. "This is bad. This is really bad."

"Is it?"

"You know, one of those guys—Joel—told me he was done. We had been together for eleven months, and the one thing I'd always told him was that I needed him to promise, if things got rough, we'd work on it together before we gave up. He agreed. He said you always needed to work on a relationship, not just walk away when things got rough."

She knew talking about her exes on a date was a huge no-no, but he was the one who insisted on making this a date when it wasn't supposed to be. She was *not* dating him. Maybe talking about her exes would get that point across to him. "But I guess he and I had other definitions of working on it, because after eleven months, he told me he was *done*. I had no idea he was unhappy at all. He never said a word. When I asked why he wasn't willing to work to try to save us, he told me he already had. He said he'd been working on it for a long time, that he'd tried everything he could think of. But I guess he forgot to tell *me* we were working on it."

Carter ran his hand down the side of her face, a caress so soft and caring, she had to turn away from it.

Instead of being put off by her talk of her ex, he pulled her in and hugged her. Didn't say anything. Didn't try to kiss her again. Didn't try platitudes or to end the non-date as awkwardly and quickly as he could. He simply held her. That made her feel foolish about everything she'd just blurted out. Here she was trying to shove him away despite the way her heart and mind were screaming at her to simply fall for the guy hard and fast And what did he do? Pulled her in tighter. He held her like that for a while before kissing her on the nose and walking her out to her car to watch as she climbed behind the wheel.

"Text me when you get home so I know you got there safe?"

Lily nodded before he shut the car door for her. She didn't know where they were headed, but she knew one thing. That was the best non-date she'd ever had.

CHAPTER EIGHT

They had three more non-dates, each one with Carter casually taking hold of her hand or putting his arm around her, bringing them closer to real dates. Each time he dropped her off at her house, he kissed her senseless and she had to spend an hour reminding herself of all the reasons not to get involved with another man who could steal her heart. She was beginning to think it was a battle that wasn't worth fighting. Because if they *were* doing battle, he was kicking her butt. She was falling hard and fast.

He'd brought her as his "non-date" to John and Katelyn's wedding, and she'd had a hard time not picturing herself up there as the happy bride someday. No matter how many times her heart had been kicked, she still wanted that. She wasn't surprised when it was Carter who flashed into her fantasy as the groom. She'd tried to push the images aside and just focus on the bride and groom of the day.

Katelyn had been absolutely radiant, surrounded by her bridesmaids. John's eyes hadn't left her the whole evening and the smile on his face told the story of their love. Lily would be lying if she said she wasn't utterly, completely envious of what they had.

"Hey guys, this is Lily Winn, the new veterinarian in town." Carter had held his hand on her lower back while he introduced Lily to the bridesmaids and groomsmen, but her traitorous heart did a little belly flop. She realized it was because she was wishing he was introducing her as *his* instead of simply the town's new veterinarian. "Lily, this is Laura and Cade Bishop, Ashley and Cora Walker, Shane Bishop, and I think you already know Danny Widen."

Lily nodded and shook hands, once again mentally smacking the crap out of the stupid feelings floating around in her belly. "It's nice to meet you all. I'm sorry I haven't been around town much at all. I haven't really had a chance to get out much with trying to get things squared away at the clinic."

Ashley smiled wide. "We'll have to come drag you out of there now that you've had a little time to settle in."

"Girls' night," Cora said with a grin, and the men rolled their eyes, but that sounded perfect to Lily. She missed her friends from school and back home. Veterinary school was intense and didn't leave a lot of time for socializing, but time with her girlfriends, even if it was only in study group, had been cherished. She hadn't realized how much burying her head in work had been costing her until now.

"That sounds perfect," she said with an answering

smile, and the group went on to chat about where she'd come from and how her grandfather was handling retirement. Throughout it all, Carter stayed close, and that stupid flip-flopping heart of hers starting doing a goofy little tap dance. *Not* what she wanted. Not at all.

And yet... Darn, there was that phrase again. She seemed to be thinking *and yet* an awful lot lately as she questioned herself at every turn. So she stopped questioning quite as much and tried to live in the moment. After getting to know several more people at the wedding reception, she let Carter take her out on the dance floor for one of the slower songs. His version of dancing was wrapping her up in those big arms of his and swaying to the music, his body pressed to hers. She didn't exactly have a problem with that. She wasn't a skilled dancer herself, and his way felt good. Really good.

She stood now in the back of her clinic and faced the truth. She was loving every minute spent with Carter. Except for the few awkward moments the night before when Ryan Crawford had seen them together in a restaurant. The angry looks Ryan had given her were hard to miss. It was all Lily could do to keep Carter from confronting him. She understood what Ryan was feeling. She'd told him she didn't date and seeing her out with Carter a short time later had to feel crappy. Maybe she could explain.

She nibbled on her bottom lip as she put a kitten back into its cage with a little scratch behind the ears. As she turned away from the kitten to scribble a few post-op notes in its record, she decided she should run over to Alton

Crawford's law firm to talk to Ryan. If she explained she and Carter weren't really dating, he would understand, wouldn't he?

Lily's phone rang, breaking the uncomfortable train of thought. "Hello," she said after pulling it out of her scrubs pocket.

"Lily? It's Mary."

The other woman's hushed tone sent a prickle of unease up her spine. "Um, hi, Mary. What's up?"

"I just talked to a few people who have heard about the dog-racing ring. They told me it's set up like a rave. People get a text an hour before a race will start with the location. It's always someplace new."

Lily actually felt her shoulders deflate. "So finding where they're being held is next to impossible."

"Not necessarily," Mary said. "I'm trying to find out the names of some of the people that attend. If we can find a name, we might get lucky and hear something about one of the races. Then we watch that person and follow them." She was whispering again and Lily understood why. What she was talking about was crazy. Crazy dangerous. Crazy stupid. But she had to admit, it might be the only way to put an end to this thing. And it sounded like it could work. *If* they could get a name, and *if* they heard any rumors about a race taking place on a certain day. Those were big ifs.

"Maybe," Lily said, not wanting to commit just yet. "I guess see what you can find out. Carter is still trying on his end. Maybe he'll be able to do something."

They had only just said their goodbyes when Carter

walked into the back area of the clinic, making Lily jump. She hadn't expected to see him today. He was on shift all day, so when he showed up in the clinic in the middle of the afternoon, her gut clenched. She hoped he hadn't overheard her and Mary talking—he would no doubt flip if he thought she might follow someone to a dog race to gather evidence. She also had a feeling he wasn't bringing her good news. His expression was too grim for that.

"Is everything okay?"

"Can we go to your office, Lily?"

She nodded and led the way, closing the door behind them.

"We found another site where we think someone was racing dogs. I don't know if it's the same group, but I suspect it is. They'd already cleared out, but we found paraphernalia and evidence of racing. Evidence they're keeping rabbits."

"Rabbits?"

His jaw was tight when he answered her. "Bait, sweetheart. They use live bait for the races."

Lily put a hand to her chest as she listened to him, feeling sick over what she was hearing. What kind of monsters would set a pack of dogs after a live bunny like that?

"Any injured dogs?" She knew he would have brought any injured ones to her, so she was essentially asking if they'd found any more dogs shot in cold blood.

"No." He shook his head and ran his hands up and down her arms as though trying to soften the blow. "None

45

this time. I have a feeling they're just moving from site to site quickly to keep one step ahead of us. It's possible they know we've started checking abandoned properties."

His explanation matched Mary's information—a new site for each race, the location texted to attendees at the last minute.

"Unfortunately, it's going to take time to catch them in the act, Lily. We don't have the budget for a big undercover sting for something like this. It's horrible, but this has to take a backseat."

Lily's temper flared. "Dead animals don't rank up there with, what, burglaries? What is it that's pulling money away from finding some sick bastard who's letting dogs tear live animals apart for sport?"

He didn't rise to her bait, and that ticked her off for a minute, too. She wanted to fight something, but he cut her argument short with his answer. "I'm sorry, Lil, but there have been a string of arsons on the other side of the county. A lot of resources are diverted there now. There are other crimes. We might not have the murder rate of bigger cities, but we do have our share of murders, assaults, things I can't pull resources from. Maybe when John comes back next week, I can talk to him and he can help me make it work, but as of right now, I'm limited in what I can do."

She bit down on the inside of her cheeks to keep from crying or yelling or lashing out in some way. It wasn't Carter's fault and he was right. Arson is serious, and she was no idiot. She knew it could lead to death too easily if someone got caught in the crossfire. But she couldn't stand the thought that there were dogs and rabbits out there being horribly mistreated. Who knew when they might decide to shoot another dog? Or hold a race and put rabbits through a horrific death for a night of gambling and so-called entertainment.

She nodded at Carter, but couldn't say anything. If she spoke, she'd end up crying in his arms, and she needed to keep it together to get through the rest of her day.

He squeezed her arms and bent to meet her eyes. "You okay, Lily? I promise, I won't give up. It's just going to take some time."

She nodded again and found her voice. "Yeah. I know. I'll be okay. At least Honey is out of their hands."

He grinned. "She's doing great. You need to come over and see her soon," he said and she smiled.

"I will. I promise."

"I have to work the next two nights, but can I cook you dinner Wednesday night." He brushed his mouth back and forth across her lips, teasing the answer he wanted from her.

She sighed into his kiss and wrapped her arms around his neck. "Yes. Dinner sounds great."

He pulled back and melted her with one of those smiles he seemed to know she couldn't deny. "So it's a date?"

She had to laugh at his raised brows and the challenge in his look. Another sigh. "Yes. It's a *date*."

As Carter walked away, Lily watched him, pulling her phone out when he'd made it through the lobby and out the front door.

See if you can get a name. She hit send and waited for

Mary to reply with an *okay* before pocketing it again. Just because Carter's hands were tied didn't mean she and Mary couldn't do all they could to stop the people responsible for this. If she could get him the proof he needed, he could take action.

CHAPTER NINE

When Mary called two days later to say she had a lead, Lily swallowed down the naysaying in her head. Carter had been clear. He needed evidence that rabbits were being killed, and more importantly, that gambling was taking place. He'd told her that the gambling was what would most likely lead to a successful prosecution. It was the more serious of the crimes being committed.

It sickened her to think that gambling might take precedence over the inhumane treatment of animals, but she could at least take action to make sure these people were stopped. So Lily didn't hesitate. Well, not for very long, anyway. Mary couldn't slip into one of the races without being noticed. People around here knew her, and they knew she lived for rescuing dogs. It wouldn't be safe for Mary.

But not many people in town knew Lily yet. If she threw her hair up under a hat and put on heavy makeup and a tight miniskirt, no one would peg her as the town veterinarian. So it was, that four hours later, she found herself at a roadside bar fifteen minutes outside of town. Not a place she would normally go, and not a place where she felt remotely safe. She tugged again at her skirt while she avoided the attentions of yet another guy in a dirty shirt with bad hair and teeth. Unfortunately, she couldn't leave. She was waiting for the man nursing a beer in the corner to get a text. Mary had told her Sonny Daigle was supposedly one of the most frequent attendees of the underground dog races. She'd heard this from a guy who knew a guy who knew a guy, and so on. Mary swore to Lily that this was good information, and a race was taking place tonight.

So when Sonny looked at his phone, then tossed a few bills on the bar and walked out, Lily did the same. She got in her car and followed him out of the lot. When Mary called a few minutes into the drive, Lily told her which way she was headed, then kept her focus on not being spotted while keeping up with Sonny. Mary called again a few minutes later, but she ignored the call. Tailing a suspect wasn't exactly something she had experience with, and it turned out it wasn't easy. At least not with her blood pounding in her veins and her palms so sweaty she thought the wheel might slip out of her grasp.

She followed him another ten minutes outside of town, all the while arguing with herself over just how stupid this actually was. Because, now that she was out in the dark alone, she recognized the immense stupidity of what she was doing. Her body seemed to recognize it, too. Everything in her screamed to turn around. To go back. Her palms were sweating and her heart felt like it would explode any minute. As a doctor, she knew it could beat that fast and not explode, but rational thought had abandoned her around the time she walked into that bar.

Around the fifteen-minute mark Lily began to feel truly panicked. It was also around that time that a truck came up behind her. The truck was only behind her for a minute before its high beams began to blind her through the rearview mirror and she could swear it was inching closer and closer to her bumper. So when Sonny's car turned off on a side road, Lily didn't have the nerve to follow. She kept going straight, planning to drive farther up the road to turn around and head back to her house. She couldn't do this. Just plain didn't have the guts to walk in there. As much as she'd hoped to get pictures or video of the people in charge, and evidence of gambling taking place, she just wasn't brave enough.

The truck stopped in front of the turn-off, looking for all the world as though it might follow her. Lily lost all ability to breathe. She gripped the steering wheel tightly and kept her eyes on the rearview mirror as she felt the first sign of tears in her eyes. This was beyond stupid. It was foolish and dangerous and she was an idiot for thinking she could do what the police couldn't do.

When the truck turned slowly down the road Sonny had gone down, she took a gulp of air, her hands shaking as she kept going straight. Forget pulling a U-turn to get home. There was no way she was going anywhere near that turn-off again. If she kept going, she'd hit another road that would take her around to the highway. She could take that home. It would take a lot longer to get home than turning back, but she could deal with that. Eyeing her rearview mirror the whole way home, Lily prayed she wouldn't see the truck or Sonny's car again.

CHAPTER TEN

L ily's hands shook as she unlocked her front door. That had to be one of the dumbest things she'd *almost* done in a long time. Okay, ever.

"*Evvvvverrrr,*" she said to herself as she bolted the door shut behind her. But at least it was over and she hadn't done it, hadn't ended up in a spot she couldn't get herself out of.

She walked into the kitchen and pulled a bottle of wine from the top shelf of her pantry. She wasn't a big drinker, but a time like this called for something to settle herself. Since she had a feeling she'd spew a shot of whiskey across the room if she ever tried to down one, she was going with wine. Wine would work. As she poured herself a glass, she thought about calling Carter. She should let him know where the race was happening. He'd said he didn't have the budget for a big investigation, but maybe he could send someone over there to check things out. Maybe they could send someone in plainclothes, or whatever you called it.

She chewed on her lower lip for a minute trying to decide if she should just text him the location or what. He'd be ticked. Well, *ticked* didn't begin to describe it. Furious, was more like it. But if that meant getting those animals away from criminals who would shoot them at the drop of a hat, it was worth Carter's wrath, right?

She sipped her wine and looked at her phone sitting on the counter. Maybe she could have Mary call him or text him? But would he listen to Mary or ignore her? If the information came from Lily, wouldn't he be more likely to believe her and get someone out there right away?

Lily picked up her phone and tapped the screen, watching it come alive.

She put it down again. Sipped her wine. Picked the phone up. Put it down.

Knock, knock, knock.

She damn near jumped out of her skin at the sound of the knock on her front door. Frozen in place for a moment, she wondered if someone might have followed her home. That was silly, though. She had watched her rearview mirror the whole ride. If someone had followed her, she would have seen them. *Right?*

She went to the front door and looked through the peephole, letting out her breath when she saw who it was. In the background, she heard her phone ringing, but she ignored it for the time being. Swinging the door open, she smiled at Ryan Crawford. She wasn't overly fond of the man, but somehow having someone with her right now seemed like a good idea. The house felt too empty. Too isolated. And she was too on edge.

"Hey, Ryan, what are you doing here?"

Relief flipped to shock when he stepped inside, shoving her into the house with one arm. He slammed the door shut behind him.

Lily didn't see the first blow coming—only felt the pain shoot through the side of her face as she fell back onto the couch. His face had gone from smiling and easygoing to ugly in the blink of an eye. Confusion and fear battled in her mind as Ryan loomed over her. Why had she ever thought he was short? He seemed to have gained inches and pounds somehow. Not to mention a whole lot of muscle and fists the size of dumbbells.

"Did you tell anyone, Lily?"

She shook her head and knew she was crying when she felt the sting of tears on her cheek. It burned, but the look in his eye told her he could do a lot worse. Cold rushed through her, but confusion came right alongside it. "Tell anyone what? I don't—"

He kneeled down in front of her, his eyes cold and hard and insanely at odds with the man she'd met in the past. She frantically tried to think of anything she could use to defend herself, but there was nothing. She didn't keep a weapon of any kind in the house, and she couldn't hope to match his strength. Her mind spun. Until he stopped it with one sentence.

"You're going to die tonight, Lily." He didn't bat an eye as he said it. Just looked at her as though the statement was completely normal, and that made her believe he meant it all the more. "Before that happens, I need to know if you told anyone the location of the dog race tonight. My dad needs to know if we have to clear the damned place out after your little stunt."

"What?" His dad? Nothing about this made any sense. And no matter how many times she shook her head, she couldn't seem to get the pieces to fall into place. Her phone rang again, sounding much too far away.

Ryan's meaty fist gripped her hair and twisted, wrenching her scalp. She raised her hands to relieve the pain, to try to stop him, but there was nothing she could do as he pulled her off the couch, dragging her through the house. "Let's go see who that is, shall we, Lily?"

CHAPTER ELEVEN

Carter tried to quell the anger in his gut as he pulled in every available deputy he could to raid the underground racing ring. No, that wasn't right. If he was honest with himself, it wasn't anger. It was fear. Fear for Lily. Fear he wouldn't be good enough to save her. He'd be damned if he'd let fear stop him, so he was stoking the anger instead.

When Mary Greene had called him in tears and told him Lily had followed Sonny Daigle out to one of the rural farm roads, he'd begun a crazed circuit from livid to terrified and back again. He'd cross checked the area with his list of abandoned properties and narrowed in on her probably location quickly. If he got her out of there safely, he'd wring her neck. Then he'd kiss the ever-loving daylights out of the woman. Then wring her neck again.

Because the other bit of information Mary had imparted was that Lily wasn't answering her phone. She'd been unresponsive for over twenty-five minutes before Mary called

Carter. There was nothing about that situation that could be good. Not a damned thing.

He scrambled to cross-reference the location with the list of abandoned properties he'd been working his way through and wasn't surprised when the one property out that way turned out to be a property the bank was in the process of seizing. The lawyer handling the case for the bank? Alton Crawford. Carter's gut had been right. Alton's interest in Honey had seemed off from the get-go.

An hour later, when they'd completed the raid, some would say the results were positive. Only one deputy had been injured, and his injuries were minor; they had seized thirty-five dogs and ten rabbits; and had detained Jenk Wilson and Alton Crawford. But they couldn't find Lily anywhere. Much as he'd like to say he was staying calm and working through the problem, Carter had to admit, he felt like he might lose it any second. He had half a mind to drag Alton Crawford off into the woods to *talk* to him one-on-one. Carter had never crossed the line in his work before, but he was preparing to blast right on through it. Because losing Lily was not an option.

"Boss."

Carter didn't bother to correct Deputy Widen, even though he felt nothing like a boss at the moment. He felt lost. He turned to the man addressing him and waited.

Widen nodded when he saw he had Carter's attention and leaned close. "We threatened to take a few of the spectators in for illegal gambling if they didn't talk. No one saw Lily. There are very few women here, so I think they would

58

have spotted her. A couple of them said Alton's son, Ryan, was here earlier and hauled ass out of the place after a lot of shouting between Ryan and Alton and Jenk. Said they started the races late because of it."

Carter nodded. "Find out what Ryan drives and call in a BOLO."

As Danny walked off to coordinate the *be on the lookout* with other law enforcement on site, Carter crossed his arms and glared at the surrounding farmland. It was a useless gesture. The landscape couldn't produce Lily safe and sound any more than Carter could, and that fact was tearing at his gut.

"Danny!" Carter shouted across the field. "Send someone over to Mary Greene's house and find out every damned thing she knows about where Lily went and who might be involved in this. And haul Sonny's ass down to the station and find out what he knows. Find out who might have seen Lily following him, and anyone and everything he saw."

CHAPTER TWELVE

L ily stood with her back to the kitchen counter, bracing herself for the next blow. Ryan was scrolling through her phone, but she knew that wouldn't keep him busy for long. Reaching behind her into the sink, she felt around for the knife she'd used at breakfast that morning. Her eyes never left Ryan as she moved her hand slowly across the sink. Part of her wanted to lie down and curl into a ball, hoping this would go away. Hoping Carter would burst through the door any minute to save her.

But a bigger part of her knew if she was going to get out of this, she had to fight. Something about the eerie calm of Ryan's demeanor told her he'd meant it when he said he planned to kill her tonight. She knew who he was and knew what he was doing. He'd assaulted and threatened her. There was no way he could let her walk out of here alive.

Her hands closed over the handle of the knife and she swallowed back a sob as she dove for Ryan. She had very little hope of winning this fight, but maybe the fact that he wouldn't expect her to attack would give her a leg up. As she came at him, he turned and raised an arm to slap her back, easy as swatting a fly. The refrigerator met her head with a violent crack as she landed.

If Lily could have slowed the scene down, she might have some idea of what happened next, but as it was, things occurred in a blur. Whether Ryan never saw the knife in her hand or simply misjudged her and didn't think she'd been able to hold onto it as she flew across the room—she simply didn't know. Time slowed as he sneered and told her she'd pay for fighting back. Instinct had her raising the knife as he threw himself toward her. The look of shocked rage on his face, mere inches from hers, would live with her forever. It would haunt her in ways she never imagined possible. She knew in that instant, she'd taken a life as the blade sank deep into his gut, his own momentum providing the power she needed.

It didn't matter that it was his life or hers. It didn't matter that the look on his face said he likely would have hurt her badly before he had killed her. That she might have wished for death when he was finished.

Lily shoved at him hard, tossing herself sideways to get out from under him as he went limp. Uncontrollable sobs wracked her body, but no sound came out. She looked down at her hands and found them shaking and bloody, but she felt detached, like she was watching someone else. She recognized the signs of shock as she began to feel numb, but wasn't functioning as a woman with medical training right now. The moment that knife struck, she'd started functioning as a victim of a horrific crime. And part of her knew, from now on she would forever be just that. A victim. She would carry this with her forevermore. And she had no one to blame but herself. She'd foolishly put herself in Ryan's crosshairs.

Lily's gaze fell to the phone that Ryan had dropped when he'd come after her. She crawled to it and cradled it to her chest before scooting into the living room. She couldn't look at the growing puddle of blood on her kitchen floor. Couldn't stomach seeing Ryan's body. Her hands shook as she dialed Carter and she desperately tried to forget the way it felt to sink a knife into another person's stomach. That feeling would never go away.

"Lily!" Carter's voice came through the line loud and clear, and she fell against the base of the couch, bringing her knees to her chest.

"I killed him." Her words weren't very clear, at least, they didn't sound clear to her.

"Where are you, sweetheart?" He sounded so calm, as though he had everything under control. She hoped he did. Hoped he would come get her, take her away from the blood.

"I'm h-home. He's dead, Carter." Another sob tore through her body and she knew she needed to get herself together, and calm herself down before she went into shock, but she didn't honestly know if she could do that.

∽

CARTER WAS MOVING to his SUV long before Lily told him where she was, motioning to Danny Widen over his shoulder. Before Danny could reach him, a chilling scream came through the line. Lily was far from safe. The relief he'd felt moments before was gone as adrenaline once again surged through him.

Danny must have heard the scream, because he was right with Carter as they hit the ground running. By the time they slammed open the doors to Carter's vehicle, Danny had radioed to one of the other men on scene to take over.

"Is anyone closer to Lily's house than we are?" Carter's voice was clipped and strained. They were only fifteen minutes from Lily's place, but that fifteen minutes could very well be too long. If she was under attack, Carter needed to get to her. Now.

"No." Danny's tone was just as grim.

CHAPTER THIRTEEN

Lily cried out as Ryan's fist slammed into her again. He leaned close to her, his breath hot in her ear, full weight pinning her to the floor as he spoke. Her blood went cold. He would follow through on his threats. He just enjoyed letting her know what was coming.

"You're going to wish to God you had killed me back there, Lily. By the time I'm through with you, you'll pray for death. Beg for it."

As he spoke, he thrust against her with his hips and she cringed, drawing a laugh from Ryan.

"I'd say this is going to be fun, but I'm afraid it's only going to be fun for me."

One arm pressed across her shoulders as he rolled to the side and reached for the belt buckle at his waist. Metal scraped metal and her stomach churned.

No!

The thought hit Lily hard and strong and she reacted

instantly. She needed to fight this. Her arms might have been pinned by her sides, but she still had some freedom of movement in her hands. Bracing, she clawed at his abdomen, searching for the spot where the knife had sunk deep earlier. When she felt the warm blood, she plunged her thumb deep before ripping as hard as she could to the right, putting everything she had into the move, knowing it was the only one she had.

The cry from Ryan was deep and guttural. He spun from her, clutching at his stomach. Lily kicked out and ran, heading for the stairs. Her breath came in jagged pants and she focused on one thing. Getting to the top. She didn't think about the fact that getting to the front or back door might have been wiser. Ryan had been between her and the front door and when she'd gotten up to run, the stairs had been right there. As she crested the top, she couldn't help but wonder if she'd end up like one of those horror movie chicks who got herself trapped instead of getting away.

Honestly, if she were watching this movie, she might have been yelling at the screen, telling herself what an idiot she was. There wasn't time for that. She could hear Ryan on the stairs behind her. She slammed into the bathroom, locking the door behind her.

Now she *knew* she was one of those stupid horror movie chicks. She'd just locked herself in a room with a very flimsy lock and nothing to use for defense. She fell to the floor, leaning her back against the door as she scanned the room. There wasn't even anything to barricade herself in with. Lily screamed and jumped when Ryan's body hit the door behind her. He was cursing with each attempted breach and his strength seemed to wane. She wanted to curl in a ball and cover her head with her hands. The window in this room was too small to climb through, even if she could climb up to it. The modern architecture had seemed charming until now, the slit of a window up near the ceiling providing light in the room, while allowing for privacy. *Brilliant.*

The sound of a siren played in the distance, but it sounded far away. Too far. Then the banging stopped, a jarring silence after the shaking of the door from Ryan's blows. Lily strained to listen, but heard nothing more than the pounding of blood in her veins and her own gulping breaths as she tried to steady her breathing. And now she did curl up. She crawled into the corner of the small room and lay on her side, her arms wrapped tight around her knees, and cried.

CHAPTER FOURTEEN

Time couldn't move fast enough as Carter and Danny entered Lily's home. He had backup coming from across town, but he and Danny couldn't wait for that. They moved in tandem as they pushed into the house. The blood damn near brought him to his knees. He could see into the open kitchen where the largest of the pools of blood began, but it didn't end there. A trail led them through the living room and up the stairs. They moved, communicating with hand signals and the shared experience of officers who had worked together in high-stakes situations before, following the trail of evidence.

When they reached the top of the steps, they found more blood outside a closed door. The sound of Lily crying reached him through the door and his heart shattered. It took all of his training to keep his head clear as he and Danny communicated. Danny covered him as Carter kicked—once, twice—as he heard Lily scream. He only prayed she was screaming because of their efforts to breach the door, not because Ryan was still in there hurting her. If he was too late...

The door gave way and Carter entered the small room, eyes finding Lily immediately. He didn't waste time, pulling her into his arms and rocking her.

"I'm here, baby. You're all right." Carter repeated the words over and over, cradling her as he listened to their backup arrive and Danny take over the scene, clearing the house with the arriving officers. Carter's hands ran over Lily. No major injuries that he could find. The blood painting the house must be Ryan's. As he took in the bruises blooming on her face, he was glad she'd made the guy bleed. He hoped she'd gutted him. The bastard had put his hands on Lily. He deserved a whole hell of a lot worse than gutting.

"No sign of him, boss," Danny reported quietly from the doorway to the bathroom. "EMTs are on the way. Two minutes out."

Carter nodded, all the while continuing to cradle the woman in his arms. The minute he'd gotten to her, he'd ceased to be on duty. He was staying with her. No way in hell he'd let her go or leave her side now.

CHAPTER FIFTEEN

Carter let his thumb play over Lily's wrist as she slept. He was trying to stay as still and quiet as he could as she rested in the hospital bed, but he needed at least one point of contact. When he'd taken stock of the scene at her house, his blood ran cold. It looked like something out of a horror movie. The thought of what could have happened to her if she hadn't been sharp enough to fight back terrified him. Where she'd found the strength, he didn't know, but he respected the hell out of her for it.

Ryan hadn't been a very large man, but he still outweighed Lily by a lot.

Lily startled awake with a sudden gasp and looked at Carter, wild-eyed. He shushed her immediately, drawing closer to hold her as she shook.

"Shh. He's gone, honey. He's not here. You're safe."

It broke his heart when she cried, but he held her, knowing she probably had to get it out. He had no idea what to say or do for her other than hold her. She knew they'd found Ryan's body. When she woke the last time, he told her his deputies had discovered Ryan's car on the shoulder of the road about three minutes from her house. He'd likely lost consciousness due to blood loss and had driven his car into a giant oak tree. The only thing that bothered Carter about the outcome was that Ryan had likely died on impact.

Carter had never considered himself a violent man, but he would have been happier with a whole lot more suffering for Ryan before death. At least he'd have the satisfaction of seeing Alton and Jenk go to trial. They were facing a slew of charges at this point, and even if they weren't convicted, Alton's career was over. Carter knew the man didn't deserve to lose his son. That wasn't something he'd wish on anyone. But another part of him knew Alton had made his bed and had to sleep in it.

And he knew if he was having this much trouble coming to terms with what had happened, Lily had to be reeling from it.

"I want to see him."

"What?" Carter pulled back and looked down at her, not sure what she was talking about. "See who?"

She swallowed. "Ryan. I want to see his body. I need to know he's gone."

"Oh, Lily." Carter didn't know what to say. His gut was screaming at him to protect her at all costs. To stop her from doing something that might haunt her. He had seen car accidents and their victims. It wasn't pretty. But his mind was telling him he needed to respect her wishes. To support her. To be there for her no matter what she needed to do to get through this. "I don't know, Lily. It's not going to be pretty. Are you sure you want that memory on top of..."

He didn't finish. He couldn't. Thinking about the memories she would need to handle damn near slayed him.

"I need to see him, Carter. I need to see he's gone, to know he can't come back. I *need* that."

He bit back a sigh and nodded. He'd take her to see Ryan's body if that's what she needed. God help him, he'd do it for her.

Lily was exhausted as Carter led her to the car. The morgue *had* been too much. But she'd needed the closure that the visit had given her. Seeing Ryan had been hard. No, more than hard. It had been disturbing on levels she couldn't even begin to describe. She was so glad Carter had been standing next to her, adding his strength to hers.

And now, as he shut the door to her side of the car and jogged around to his, it dawned on her. She had no place to go. Her grandfather had recently moved to a nursing home, so staying with him wasn't an option. She couldn't go to her place. Even if she got the blood cleaned up, she would still see it. She would know that it had covered the walls, floors, and everything else in there the day before. She couldn't face that.

She supposed she could go to the clinic. She had a small couch in the employee lounge. It would be a bit awkward when her employees figured out she was living in the back room, but what choice did she have?

"Can you drop me off at the clinic?"

The look he gave her would have been comical in any other situation. "No."

"No?"

"No. I'll take you to my house until you find a new place."

Lily felt tears battling to break through, but she clawed at her resolve to keep them from falling. She wouldn't let this throw her and Carter together in a way they weren't ready for yet. She was hurt and vulnerable and scared senseless, but that didn't mean she should compound the problems she was facing by letting herself trust this guy. By letting herself believe that they were more than they were. Letting herself believe in *them*. She knew better than that.

Carter eyed her as he steered the car to the side of the road, stopping on the shoulder. Lily kept her eyes pinned to the windshield. She wouldn't let him talk her into this. She couldn't. She just couldn't believe in a man again and have him leave. As if reading her mind, he began talking.

"I'm not going to tell you I'm not leaving. I won't tell you I love you or say I need commitment from you. I won't ask you to believe in me or believe in us, Lily."

He paused and she had to battle the urge to turn and look at him as she felt a tear slide down her cheek. She ignored it. She locked onto the road in front of her and clamped her hands together in her lap.

He threaded his hand through her hair and gently

turned her to look at him. "I'll *show* you, Lily. Every day. I'll just show up every damned day and be there for you, be *with* you. Two, three, four years from now, if I'm lucky, you'll know I'm not going away."

Lily felt like she might hyperventilate, but she looked into his eyes and let herself fall. Maybe it wasn't so much that she let herself. It was more like she acknowledged there wasn't any use fighting anymore. She'd fallen for him, heart, body, and soul, long before this.

He didn't wait for her to answer. Just pressed a soft kiss to her mouth, then turned and started the car again. "We can look for a new place for you in the morning. For now, you'll be safe at my place and I'll sleep better knowing I'm there if you wake up with a bad dream."

His gaze held hers and he slowly slid his hand to the nape of her neck. The sensation danced up her spine, then zinged through her body as his lips found hers. Soft at first, just a little pressure. When her hands found his shoulders, he murmured and pulled her closer, and her body responded as though he'd laid her down and stripped her. He nipped and teased and she melted into the kiss, wanting more, and knowing he'd give her just what she needed. He would wait, too, if she asked him to. That knowledge was empowering. It seemed to unlock a piece of her, letting her believe. Letting her have the faith she needed if she was going to stop being a slave to the men who'd left her behind. Stop being a slave to their memories.

When Carter pulled back, she felt his absence, but the seductive look in his eyes told her the separation wouldn't be a long one. He turned without a word and put the car in gear. Lily watched his profile as he drove, loving that he wasn't pushing her to move in simply because circumstances said she needed a place to stay for a while. He was giving her what she needed—assurance that he wasn't going to push her to make this arrangement permanent before she was ready for it. But that's the way he was. He *got* her. He understood what she needed, often before she even knew she needed it. She took a deep breath and wiped the tears from her cheeks. She didn't think there would be more tears tonight. She was done crying for a while.

She let herself trust. She let herself live in the moment and know, for now, it was okay to rely on Carter. To rely on the strength of them together. The breath she took in that moment felt deeper, better, than any she'd felt in a long time. In that moment, Lily knew she didn't want to live in the shadows of the past. Just because her exes had left, didn't mean she should never trust again. She wouldn't live a half-life any longer. She'd let herself believe in Carter and the happiness they could have together from this point on. If it didn't last, she'd deal with that later. But she wouldn't live in fear any longer.

Lily took Carter's hand as he drove, and he turned to throw a quick wink and smile her way before focusing on the road. She let the smile that came from deep in her heart break free. Today was a good day. And that was what mattered right now. Today.

❧

I HOPE you guys loved this little short! Racing greyhounds are near and dear to my heart, so I wanted to feature them in a book. Next up, Cade's brother, Shane Bishop, gets his turn! I know you've been waiting to see what happened to him. Well, let me just say, that buttoned-up lawyer met his match. Grab Desire and Protect here! loriryanromance.-com/book/Desire-and-Protect

Read on for chapter one of Desire and Protect:

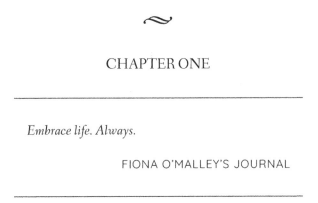

CHAPTER ONE

Embrace life. Always.

FIONA O'MALLEY'S JOURNAL

THIS WAS GOING POORLY. Then again, what had she expected? Phoebe Joy had given a lot of thought to the town she wanted to settle in, but not a single thought in the world to whether there would be a job for her there when she did.

So, here she was, applying for a job as a paralegal. This was the new Phoebe Joy.

She'd gotten her degree in paralegal studies years before to appease her father, but she hadn't ever used it. She'd dusted off that bad boy and hit the wanted ads with a vengeance. And now, armed with said paralegal degree and really very little else, she sat in the law office of Shane J. Bishop, Attorney-at-Law, trying not to squirm in her seat as the suited man read her résumé.

She was forcing herself to ignore the fact that he didn't look at all like she'd thought he would. When she thought small town lawyer, she thought of white hair and wire rimmed glasses. Or a large belly that said he spent too much time sitting in front of a computer. This man, well, he had none of that. He was tall, dark, and troubling. Troubling because the tall and dark part was all put together too damned well. Dark hair, dark eyes, chiseled jaw.

Phoebe shook her head to clear the thoughts and reminded herself she was supposed to be ignoring all of that.

He glanced up at her, scowled, then looked back at her résumé.

Just as she thought. No one was going to take her seriously. Her name had set her up for that years ago. Who names a baby Phoebe Joy? If your last name is Joy, your parents really should come up with a very serious name to go with it, like Susan or Jill.

Phoebe frowned. Jill doesn't work. Jill Joy is no good. Jane doesn't work either. Susan isn't horrible. Susan Joy. That could work. Suzanne might be even better.

But, Phoebe Joy. That had set her up. No one can take anyone named Phoebe Joy seriously. There was a time when she'd have liked that. She hadn't wanted to be taken overly seriously. But things were different now.

Her dad could have changed it at any point after her

mom had left. Someday, she'd need to ask why he hadn't. His last name was Brophy. Why hadn't he changed her name to Phoebe Brophy? She supposed she could have done the same at some point in the eleven years since she'd turned eighteen.

Or better, she could have gone back to the original French spelling of the name: Joie. That would have worked. Not that she knew anything about her mother's ancestry or the family name. Or the entire family, for that matter. She'd simply looked it up on ancestry.com one day.

"So, uh, Ms. Joy. It looks like you've had several jobs since you received your degree, none of which have been in any way related to paralegal studies." He did have a way of putting rather a fine point on things, didn't he? She glued her bottom to the seat and refused to squirm.

"Is that a question?" *Oh crap. That's probably not a good way to start an interview.* She tried again. "I mean, no. I haven't used my paralegal degree yet. I've been doing other things." *Brilliant. Just brilliant, Phoebe.*

"Yes, I can see that. You spent a year scooping ice cream at Ben's Old-Fashioned Scoops, two years as a receptionist at Ray's Tattoo and Piercing Pagoda, two years at a paint-your-own pottery studio, and..." He glanced up at her briefly before lowering his eyes to the page again. "A month? A month at a pet store cleaning out the animal cages?"

"I've included references from all of them," Phoebe smiled, wondering briefly why on earth she'd put the one month stint at the pet store on there. How do you explain to someone that you've spent several years of your adult life being a free spirit, only to realize that's not what you want? What you want is stability, a home, a family, a decent steadfast man to come home to? Like the one sitting in front of her.

Shut up, Phoebe.

"Yes," he nodded, "I can see that. Excellent references from all of them, in fact. They all have wonderful things to say about you. Including Ray, the tattoo artist who 'hopes you'll come back to him someday and make an honest man of him'."

Was it her imagination or did Shane Bishop just flinch at the exact moment that she had? Can you call jinx on a flinch? Because if you could, maybe she could get a free soda out of this interview at the very least.

She'd spent several years hiking and traveling. She'd thought about putting that on her résumé, but hiking the Appalachian Trail and living off your dad while you found yourself wasn't really anything to recommend her, was it? She'd been happy with her vagabond ways. Her dad, on the other hand, well...he'd had higher aspirations in mind. She and her father had finally come up with a deal. She'd get her paralegal degree and then she could either choose to use it or not. She chose not. Until now.

She wondered if she should simply end the interview before things went any further down the proverbial hill. No. That wasn't like her. She might be considered flighty by many people, but she wasn't a quitter. Well, the pet store... she'd quit that. But that was because she'd been about to be fired. When your boss caught you trying to let all twelve of the store's tortoises slip out the door to freedom, you had very little say in the matter. It was quit or be fired.

As it turned out, her boss had been tempted to do the same himself. He'd been almost apologetic in telling her she was going to be fired if she didn't leave on her own. It was why he continued giving her glowing recommendations despite the incident.

The other references had all been earned the honest way. She'd made herself indispensable. It was one of the things her dad had drilled into her. You work hard, take initiative, and make yourself indispensable, so that if you ever leave, it's your own choice. And if you ever need a raise, he'd say with a laugh, that's your own choice, too.

Phoebe raised her chin and plowed forward. "I wanted to spend some time gaining experience before putting my paralegal degree to work. I traveled some, worked with a wide range of people, and—" she gestured toward the résumé "—gained valuable management and customer relations experience at each of the positions I held."

She mentally crossed her fingers behind her back. She hadn't attained anything of the sort at the pet store. It was the one exception.

She hoped he couldn't see through her. The truth was she had been floating for the last few years. Of course, she hadn't realized it at the time. As it turned out, she wasn't always the most aware person in the world. Take, for example, her latest relationship.

She'd spent eighteen months with Michael Williams.

Eighteen months where she thought they were building something, heading somewhere. It had taken a single afternoon at a friend's wedding to nip that fantasy in the bud.

SHANE BISHOP STARED at the woman in front of him. She wore a black pantsuit with the smallest hint of a bright purple blouse beneath it. She didn't need to wear a suit to the office any more than he did. He should really consider dressing down on days he didn't need to go to court. Her hair looked as if it would like to wrestle itself out of the pins and ties she'd used to put it back in a twist. Blonde curls peeked out at the edges of her heart-shaped face and he had the bizarre urge to tell her she didn't need to wear it pinned up, either.

The truth was, she could pretty much dictate her terms. Her salary, hours, and wardrobe were all open to negotiation. What wasn't open to negotiation was whether he would hire her. Despite the fact that her résumé offered a strange hodge-podge of experience, none of which was related to the law, she was the most qualified applicant he'd had since his last paralegal had left town six months ago.

Evers, Texas, was a small place. It might be growing dramatically, but it still wasn't a big city. There was a growing artist population, but you had to drive thirty minutes to get to a movie theater and there weren't any concerts or anything bigger than small local theater productions.

A lot of people didn't want to stay. He needed to make sure she did. He'd had only two other applicants; Mrs. Steinecker, who could no longer hear but refused to get a hearing aid, and a man who wanted to know if it would be acceptable to be nude around the office, provided they didn't have any clients coming in that day.

"How soon would you be able to start?" he asked. The shock on her face when she turned back to him was amusing, but Shane kept the humor from showing on his face.

"Um, Monday? I could begin Monday, if you'd like," she said, confusion making her eyebrows knit together and the cupid bow of her lips purse up.

Distraction. That was the one thing he thought of when he looked at Phoebe Joy. She was going to be a distraction. On the other hand, maybe she'd be able to help him get caught up. He looked at the work piled in his inbox. It seemed like the pile hadn't gotten any smaller in recent months.

He looked back to Ms. Joy with a nod. "Good. I'll see you Monday, then."

"Oh." She said this with a bit of shock and he found himself fighting a smile for the second time. If nothing else, she'd entertain him. Lord, he hoped she did more than that, though. He needed someone competent.

They tied up the details and she walked out.

Shane walked to the low chest of filing cabinets that fronted his window and began flicking through the files he'd stacked there. A flash of pink—well, what he thought of as pink but had once been informed was peach—caught his eye out the window. Mindy Mason waved at him as she crossed the lawn to the library. He raised his hand in a wave but didn't smile. If he was too friendly, he'd learned, she would come over to talk and he'd never be rid of her.

Mindy Mason was one of what he thought of in his head as the Sweater Sets. He frowned to himself as he looked back down at the folder. There were three of them in town and there was a time he'd thought he'd marry one of the Sweater Sets. Unfortunately, it turned out, they'd all bored him to tears.

"Sweater sets. So damned tired of peach sweater sets," Shane mumbled under his breath. He didn't hear the door to his office open. "Why are they always peach, anyway?" He thought of the bright purple blouse hiding under Phoebe Joy's suit, but shoved the thought aside right away. Not only was she not the right kind of woman for him, she was his employee. Or she would be on Monday, anyway.

The Sweater Sets were supposed to be the right kind of woman for him. He grimaced.

"Why are what always peach?" Cade's voice came right behind him, causing Shane to jump a foot, which had to have been Cade's intention.

"Funny, little brother." Shane grabbed a stack of papers from a nearby table and sat at his desk. If he looked busy enough, he could get Cade out of there and get back to figuring out what it was about Phoebe Joy that had gotten under his skin. "My new paralegal doesn't start until Monday and I've got a pile of work to get through. Did you need something?"

"Wow. Sorry. Moody, huh? You want me to have Mama run some Midol and an apple pie or something over for you?" Cade asked, kicking his feet up onto the desk and ignoring the look Shane sent his way. Cade might be the more laid back of the two brothers, but he did like egging Shane on.

Shane just glared at him. He'd found staying quiet when Cade was in one of these moods was usually his best bet. In fact, it was the best way to flip the situation and irritate Cade.

"Oh, wow, was it the beautiful woman who just left your office that has you all in a snit?" Cade asked.

Apparently, no strategy was going to stop Cade today.

"That beautiful woman—happily-married brother of mine—is my new paralegal."

"Very happily married, you might add. Doesn't mean I don't take note when a beautiful woman gets my brother's boxers all in a bunch," Cade said, an all-too-smug grin firmly planted on his face. "Well, I'll tell Ma you'll be making it to Sunday dinners again now that you've finally hired someone to help you here. That's actually the reason I'm here. She sent me to tell you if you didn't make it this Sunday, she'd skin you and serve you for next week's dinner. I thought that was pretty gross, but I wasn't about to argue with her. She's been in a bad mood since you started missing dinners three months back."

Shane grunted. He wouldn't be any more caught up on Sunday than he was now, but at least he'd have help starting Monday. Just what kind of help that would be, he had no idea. He caught himself looking at the door again, thinking about the woman who'd just left. Hiring her might have been a big mistake. What little help she'd probably be with no experience in law couldn't possibly make up for the enormous distraction she was. Shane pulled his eyes away and refocused on Cade—who was still grinning like a damn Cheshire cat.

"What?" Shane demanded.

Cade laughed and shook his head. "Oh, nothing, Big Brother. Nothing at all."

GET DESIRE AND PROTECT HERE! loriryanromance.com/book/Desire-and-Protect

ABOUT THE AUTHOR

Lori Ryan is a NY Times and USA Today bestselling author who writes romantic suspense, contemporary romance, and sports romance. She lives with an extremely understanding husband, three wonderful children, and two mostly-behaved dogs in Austin, Texas. It's a bit of a zoo, but she wouldn't change a thing.

Lori published her first novel in April of 2013 and hasn't looked back since then. She loves to connect with her readers.

For new release info and bonus content, join her newslettter here: loriryanromance.com/lets-keep-touch.

Follow her online:

facebook.com/loriryanromance

twitter.com/Loriryanauthor

instagram.com/loriryanauthor